D0471425
E
Petty
Copy 1
Petty, Kate
Stop, look and
listen, Mr. Toad!
8.95
DATE DUE
SE 08 '94
SE 09 '10
NOV 29 1997
OCT 26 2002
FE 16 '08
Round Valley
Public Library
P. O. Box 620
Covelo, CA 95428

First edition for the United States, Canada,
and the Philippines published 1991
by Barron's Educational Series, Inc.

Design David West Children's Book Design

Designed and produced by
Aladdin Books Ltd
28 Percy Street
London W1P 9FF

All inquiries should be addressed to:
Barron's Educational Series, Inc.
250 Wireless Boulevard
Hauppauge, NY 11788

International Standard Book No. 0-8120-6230-2

Library of Congress Catalog Card No. 91-14214

Library of Congress Cataloging-in Publication Data

Petty, Kate.
Stop, look and listen Mr. Toad!/Kate Petty: illustrations
by Alan Baker.
p. cm.
Summary: Splendidly warty Mr. Toad wakes up from his
winter nap, makes his way to the pond, and finds a wife.
ISBN 0-8120-6230-2
[1. Toads — Fiction.] I. Baker, Alan. ill. II. Title.
PZ7.P44814Sto 1991
[E] — dc20

Printed in Belgium

1234 987654321

Stop, Look and Listen, Mr. Toad!

Kate Petty
Illustrations by Alan Baker

BARRON'S
New York · Toronto

The assistance of the National Safety Council in reviewing the safety advice in this book is gratefully acknowledged.

Mr. Toad has had a very long nap.
He's been asleep all winter.
Wake up, Mr. Toad. It's spring.

Mr. Toad opens his right eye
and shuts it again.
He opens his left eye
and shuts it again.

Too early.
"I don't get up until sundown."

In the gentle light of evening
Mr. Toad starts to get up.
He yawns. He stretches.

He looks in the mirror.
"Ah. What a splendidly warty fellow I am,"
thinks Mr. Toad. "Time to get all dressed up."

Suddenly Mr. Toad remembers
what he has to do today.
"That's it. I must go back to my pond
and find myself a wife."

That shouldn't be too hard
for a splendidly warty fellow
like Mr. Toad.
He puts on his finest clothes.

Breakfast first.
"Watch out breakfast, here I come."

With a flick of his tongue
Mr. Toad catches a delicious beetle.

And a scrumptious flying ant.

And a mouth-watering worm.
"That's better. Now I'm ready for anything."

Mr. Toad sets off across the fields,
walking in a leisurely sort of way.
"Wouldn't catch me leaping around
like a ridiculous frog," thinks Mr. Toad.

But it is a long way to the pond.
Mr. Toad croaks a little song
to keep his spirits up.

"Over hill and over dale,
across the fields, across the vale…"
Mr. Toad stops.
He hears a noise.

Whoosh. Whoosh. Whoosh.
Bright beams of light
cut through the dark.
Mr. Toad has reached the road.

He can't go around it.
He can't go under it.
He'll just have to go across it.

Mr. Toad tries to remember all he's learned about crossing roads.

"Look right, look left, look up? No. That's not it. Look, listen, whistle, sing – that's not it."

Think, Mr. Toad.

But poor Mr. Toad is dazzled by the lights.
He can't think straight.
Now. **WATCH OUT**.

Mr. Toad leaps back to safety.
That was close.
He was very nearly squashed.

Mr. Toad squats down
and holds his head in his hands.

Oh dear. He'll never cross the road tonight.
And he'll never get to the pond.
And he'll never find a wife.
But what's that? *Listen*, Mr. Toad.

Crroak...crroak...crroak.
Mr. Toad follows the sound.
Oh, look. There are all his old friends.
Even the lovely Miss Lumpy.

Miss Lumpy is pleased to see Mr. Toad.

She thinks he's looking splendidly warty.

So many toads.
They look for a safe place to cross.
They stop near the curb.
They look left, right and left again.
They listen carefully.
They wait until the road is clear.
Then they walk straight across.
They keep looking and listening
all the way.

They reach the other side safely.
And there's the pond.
Mr. Toad has arrived there at last.
He's even found himself a wife.

Mr. Toad and Miss Lumpy
get married in the moonlight.
And before long

they have a very large family indeed.

Don't be like Mr. Toad. Follow these rules and cross the road safely.

Always cross with a grown-up and hold hands while crossing.

Find the safest place to cross — either at a crosswalk or well away from parked cars that can hide oncoming traffic. Do not cross near any bends in the road so that you can clearly see if any cars are coming.

Stop at the curb.
Look left, right, and left again.
Listen for traffic.
When it is safe to cross, walk straight across the road.
Do not run.
Keep looking and listening for traffic while you cross.